With huge appreciation
for the 'Honest' family
(sometimes known as Clark)
J. B.

To Mum and Dad
L. C.

First published in 2000 in Great Britain by David & Charles Children's Books,
Published in this edition in 2006 by
Gullane Children's Books
an imprint of Pinwheel Limited
Winchester House, 259-269 Old Marylebone Road,
London NW1 5XJ

Text © Jemma Beeke 2000
Illustrations © Lynne Chapman 2000

ISBN-13: 978-1-86233-633-9
ISBN-10: 1-86233-633-4

Printed and bound in Singapore

This book
belongs to

_____

_____

The Show at
RICKETY BARN

Written by Jemma Beeke
Illustrated by Lynne Chapman

GULLANE
CHILDREN'S BOOKS

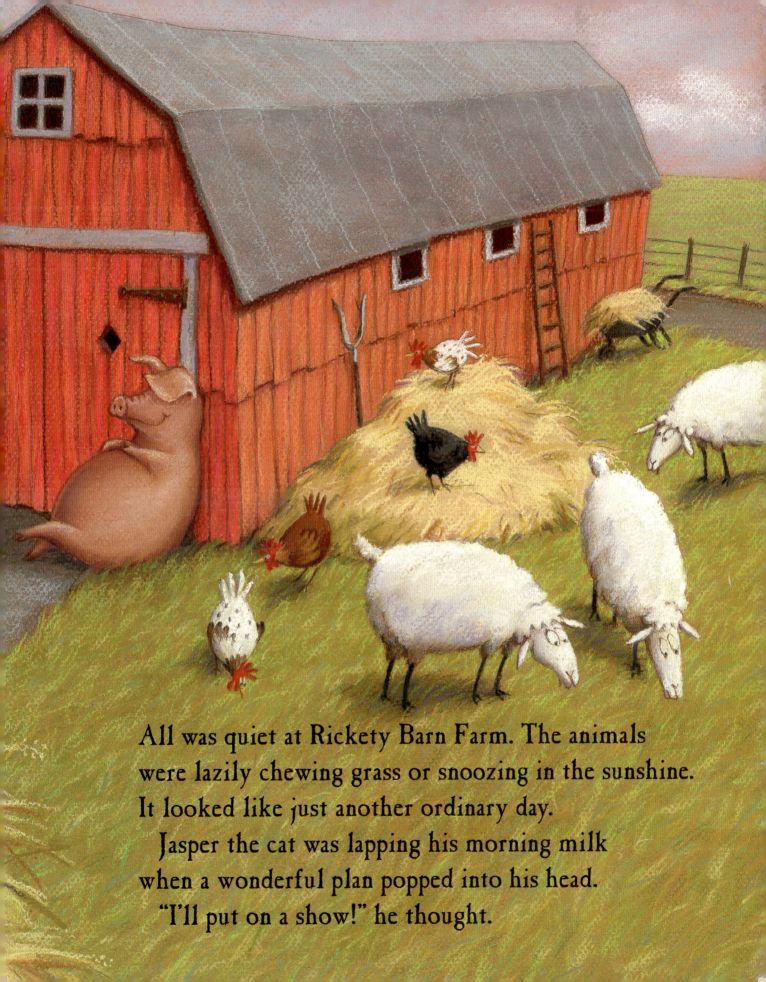

All was quiet at Rickety Barn Farm. The animals
were lazily chewing grass or snoozing in the sunshine.
It looked like just another ordinary day.

Jasper the cat was lapping his morning milk
when a wonderful plan popped into his head.

"I'll put on a show!" he thought.

He made a huge poster to pin
on the door of the rickety barn.
"There!" he said to himself. "All the
other animals will love my performance."

Jasper thought he had better
start practising straight away.

"Why are you singing?" asked Sniggle the pig, as he passed by.
Jasper whispered in his ear, "I'm getting ready for the show."

"Show? What show?" squealed Sniggle loudly.
"Shhh! The Rickety Barn Show, of course," Jasper replied grandly.
"How exciting," said Sniggle. "Might a pig be in it too?"

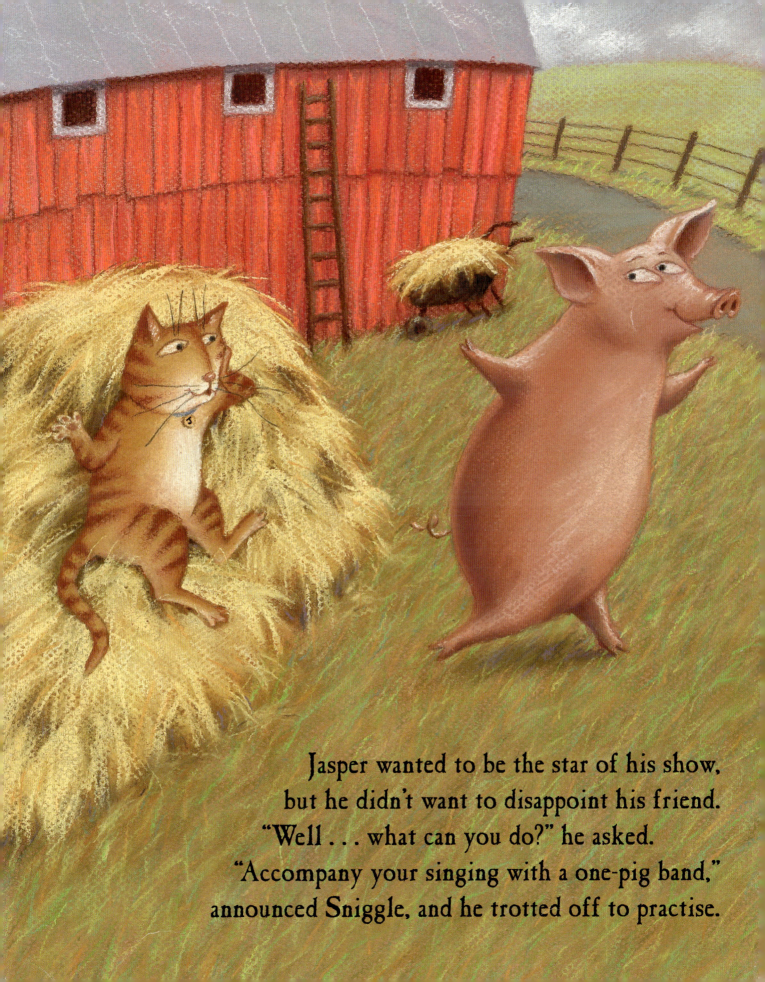

Jasper wanted to be the star of his show,
but he didn't want to disappoint his friend.
"Well . . . what can you do?" he asked.
"Accompany your singing with a one-pig band,"
announced Sniggle, and he trotted off to practise.

"Why are you toot-tooting on that bugle?" asked Suzie the hen.

"I'm getting ready for the show," Sniggle whispered. **"Show? What show?"** clucked Suzie in excitement. "The Rickety Barn Show, what else!" declared Sniggle.

"Can we hens be
in it too?" pleaded Suzie.
"Well . . . what can you do?" Sniggle asked.
"Dance along to the band!" cried Suzie.
And she rushed off to tell the others.

"What's all this rowdy nonsense?"
Austin the old cart-horse enquired bossily.

"We're getting ready for the show," bragged Suzie.

"Show? What show?" Austin asked
with a rare whinny of excitement.

"The Rickety Barn Show, of course!"
chorused the hens joyfully.

"Sounds delightful," said Austin.
"I'd like to offer my services."
"Well . . . what can you do?" Suzie asked Austin.
"Bring an air of dignity to the proceedings," he announced.
"I will be reading a short poem that I have written specially."
And he plodded off to practise.

Flora the sheep appeared.

"Great poem, Austin! But why are you reading it to yourself?" Flora asked.

Austin looked around with a superior air.

"I'm getting ready for the show," he declared.

"Show? What show?" bleated Flora loudly.

Oh littl
upon

La-dee-dah!

TOOT! TOOT! TOOT!

♪ ♫ Miiaaoow!

flower
the ground...

"The Rickety Barn Show, of course," replied Austin stuffily.
"How maaaaarvellous. Can we sheep be in it too?" pleaded Flora.
"Well . . ." Austin pondered. "What can you do?"
"An acrobatics display," announced Flora,
as she skipped away to tell the others.

"Yoo-hoo! What's happening?"
mooed Chloe the cow.
"We're getting ready for the show!"
called Flora from the top of
the swaying pyramid.

"Show? What show?"
asked Chloe.

"Haven't you heard? The Rickety Ba-aarn Show!"
replied all the sheep together.
"Oooo, what fun! Can the cows be in it too?" pleaded Chloe.
"Ma-a-aybe . . . what can you do?" Flora asked.
"Perform a juggling act," boasted Chloe,
and she hurried off to tell the others.

"Why are you throwing things around?" gasped
Bruce the sheepdog, as plates crashed around him.
"We're getting ready for the show," replied Chloe.

"Show? What show?" he demanded.
"The Rickety Barn Show! What else!" replied the cows.
"Well, you can't have a show without a host," advised Bruce.
"Oh . . ." said Chloe, because there wasn't much else to say.

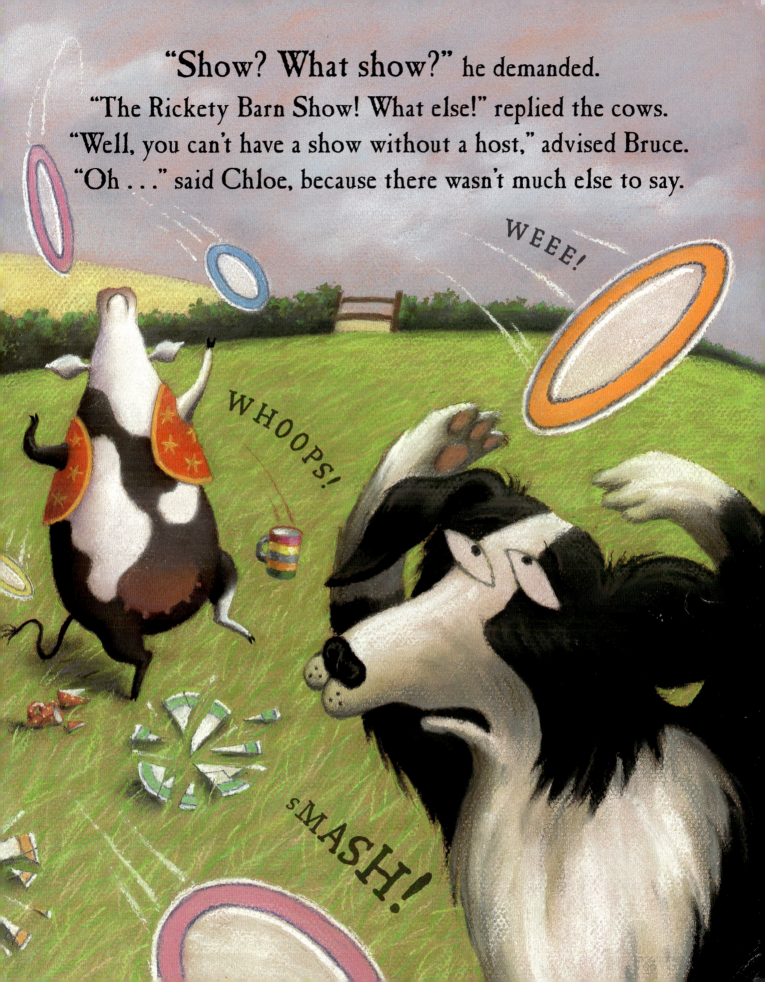

Just before three o'clock, all the performers gathered in the rickety barn. Bruce stood by the door to welcome the audience, and the other animals huddled nervously behind the hay bales.

Rickety Barn
SHOW
today
t 3 o'c
everybod
welcome

At three o'clock,
nobody had arrived
to watch the show.

By five past three,
the animals were starting
to shuffle their feet.

By ten past three,
still nobody had come
through the door
of the rickety barn.

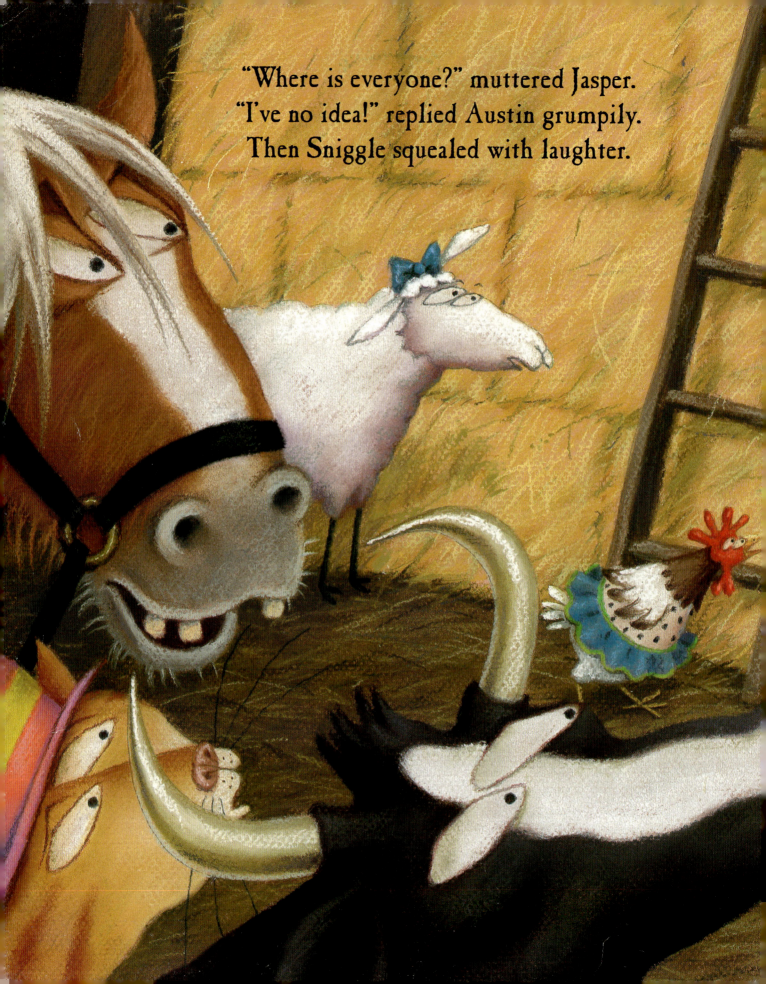

"Where is everyone?" muttered Jasper.
"I've no idea!" replied Austin grumpily.
Then Sniggle squealed with laughter.

The others gave him a puzzled look.
"There's nobody to watch the show,"
he laughed, "because . . .

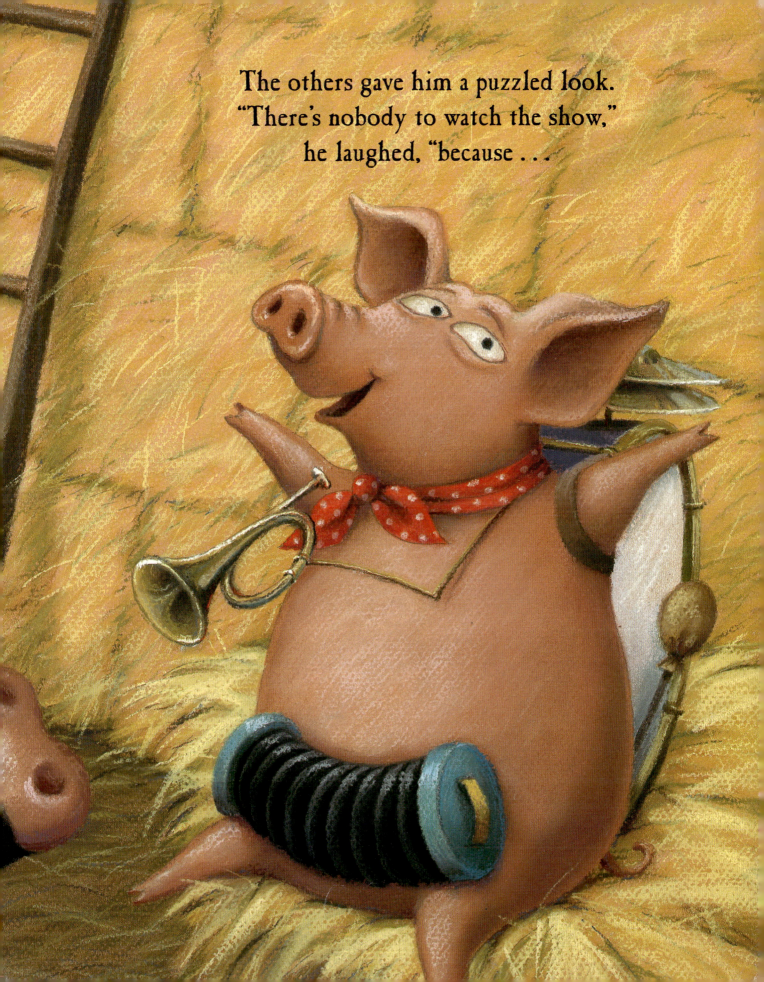

...We're all in it!"
There was only one thing to do.
"The show must go on!"
cried Jasper.
And it did.

How to put on a
RICKETY BARN SHOW

Tell your friends that you're going to put on
a Rickety Barn Show. Ask everyone to perform something
they like: singing, playing an instrument, dancing or reading
poetry, for example. Ask who would like to be the show host.

You could then make your own snazzy invitations and hand them
out to those friends who you'd like to be in the audience.

Choose your costumes and prepare for
your performance together!

Make fun show leaflets for the audience, listing
the time and place and who will be performing.

Ask an adult if they could help you
make some show snacks, such as popcorn.

The show host can now announce the
beginning of your fabulous

Rickety Barn Show!

Other Gullane Children's Books
illustrated by Lynne Chapman . . .

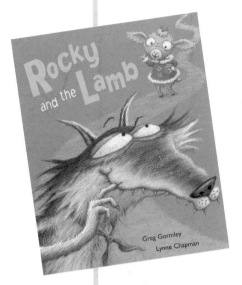

Rocky and the Lamb
GREG GORMLEY (AUTHOR)

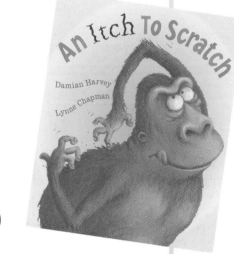

An Itch to Scratch
DAMIAN HARVEY (AUTHOR)

Big Bad Wolf is Good
SIMON PUTTOCK (AUTHOR)

**A New House
for Smudge**
MIRIAM MOSS (AUTHOR)